RUNNING WILD

J.G. Ballard was born in Shanghai in 1930 and was interned by the Japanese from 1942 to 1945, an experience reflected in *Empire of the Sun*, which was shortlisted for the Booker Prize and the James Tait Black Memorial Prize. He has also written *Myths of The Near Future*, *The Unlimited Dream Company*, and *The Day of Creation*.

A R E N A
N O V E L L A

RUNNING WILD
J.G. Ballard

ARENA
NOVELLA

An Arena Book
Published by Arrow Books Limited
62–65 Chandos Place, London WC2N 4NW

An imprint of Century Hutchinson Limited

London Melbourne Sydney Auckland
Johannesburg and agencies throughout
the world

First published in Great Britain in 1988 by
Century Hutchinson Ltd in the Hutchinson Novellas series

Arena Edition 1989

© J.G. Ballard 1988

Typeset in Monophoto Photina by
Vision Typesetting, Manchester

Printed and bound in Great Britain by
The Guernsey Press, Co. Ltd,
Guernsey, C. I.

ISBN 0 09 973050 2

25 August 1988. Where to start? So much has been written about the Pangbourne Massacre, as it is now known in the popular press throughout the world, that I find it difficult to see this tragic event with a clear eye. In the past two months there have been so many television programmes about the 32 murdered residents of this exclusive estate to the west of London, and so much speculation about the abduction of their 13 children, that there scarcely seems room for even a single fresh hypothesis.

However, as the Permanent Secretary impressed upon me at the Home Office this morning, virtually nothing is known about the motives and identity of the assassins.

'I say "assassins", Doctor Greville, but there may have been only one of them. I'm told that some sort of martial arts fanatic could have got away with it.' Sitting beneath the portrait of his more illustrious predecessor, he gestured gloomily. 'And as for the whereabouts of the orphaned children – they've vanished through some window in time and space. Not a ransom demand, or even a simple threat to kill them . . .'

He sounded almost aggrieved, and I commented: 'All the same, I think we should assume that they're still alive.'

'Should we? To be honest, doctor, I'd rather you didn't assume anything. That's why I've asked you here.'

He stared at me without hope, already regretting the decision. As we both well knew, the fact that I had been called in by the Home Office, after my unpopular minority report on the Hungerford killings, was less a compliment to me than a comment on the failure of the police, the CID and the intelligence services to come up with even a solitary clue to the sources of this horrific crime.

As baffled as the Permanent Secretary, I could only think of asking his permission to visit the murder site at Pangbourne Village. The luxury housing estate was still sealed off from the press and public, but had been tramped over by an army of heavy-footed investigators. I waited as he scribbled my *laissez-passer*, my arms burdened by two Home Office briefcases loaded with their probably useless files. Then I remembered the comfortable seats of the viewing theatre in the Whitehall basement, and as an afterthought asked if I could see the police video recorded at Pangbourne within a few hours of the crime.

'The police video? All right, but it's pretty grim stuff. Though after Hungerford, I dare say you have the stomach for this sort of thing, doctor . . .'

Irritated by his tone, I almost declined. The senior people at both the Home Office and Scotland Yard regarded me as a dangerous maverick, overly prone to lateral thinking and liable to come up with one embarrassing discovery after another. Later, looking back as I revise these diaries for publication, I realize that it was there, in the deserted viewing theatre, that I was given my first glimpse into the real causes of the Pangbourne Massacre. If I failed to recognize what I saw, and if over the course of my investigation I seem unduly slow to identify the culprits, I can only plead that what now appears self-evident scarcely seemed so at the time. My failure to recognise the obvious, in common with almost everyone else concerned, is a measure of the true mystery of the Pangbourne Massacre.

The Police Video
Like millions of other television viewers, I had already seen selected extracts from the film in numerous documentaries about the massacre, and I hardly expected any sudden revelation. But as I relaxed in the viewing theatre, I soon realized what a remarkable film this was, and how well it conveyed the curious atmosphere of Pangbourne Village – in its elegant and civilized way a scene-of-the-crime waiting for its murder.

The 28-minute film was taken by officers of Reading CID soon after eleven o'clock on the morning of 25 June 1988, some three hours after the murders. Thankfully, there is no sound-track, and one is glad that none is necessary, unlike the TV programmes with their hectoring commentaries full of lurid speculation. This minimalist style of camera-work exactly suits the subject matter, the shadowless summer sunlight and the almost blank facades of the expensive houses – everything is strangely blanched, drained of all emotion, and one seems to be visiting a set of laboratories in a high-tech science park where no human operatives are employed.

The film opens by the gatehouse that controlled access to the ten mansions, the recreation club and gymnasium that made up the estate. The medallion of the private security firm is visible beside the visitors' microphone, but there is no sign of the uniformed security guard who usually sat at the window.

The camera turns to show the delivery van of the local wine-merchants which the police have parked among the ornamental trees on the grass verge. The driver, a pallid young man in his early twenties, is staring in a despondent way at the deep ruts left in the finely trimmed grass, as if the costs of restoring this once-immaculate surface will have to be met from his wages. It was he who gave the alarm, after discovering the first of the bodies as he delivered a case of white Burgundy to the Garfield house (no. 3, The Avenue).

The camera fixes on him, and like a badly trained actor he steps forward to the gatehouse, a tic jumping across his sallow cheek. He points to the door, and a uniformed constable opens the armoured glass panel to reveal the interior of the office.

A security guard is lying on the floor below the row of television monitors, their screens a blizzard of snow. Someone has cut the cable running from the surveillance cameras mounted all over the estate, but clearly officer Turner had no time to reach for the telephone whose scissored cord hangs from the desk above his head. Arms pinioned, he lies within a bizarre contraption of rope and bamboo sticks, his neck gripped by a pair of spring-loaded steel calipers, as if in his bored moments he had been constructing a box-kite for one of the pampered children of the estate and had been trapped inside it.

In fact, as I can see from the livid contusions on his larynx, he has strangled himself after blundering into this lethal cat's cradle which his murderer dropped over his shoulders, its double nooses tightening around his neck as he struggled to free his arms and legs.

The camera leaves the gatehouse and sets off along The Avenue, the tree-lined central drive of the estate. The handsome mansions sit above their ample front lawns, separated from each other by screens of ornamental shrubs and dry-stone walls. The light is flat but remarkably even, a consequence of the generous zoning densities (approx. two acres per house) and the absence of those cheap silver firs which cast their bleak shadows across the mock-Tudor facades of so many executive estates in the Thames Valley.

As well, though, there is an antiseptic quality about Pangbourne Village, as if these company directors, financiers and television tycoons have succeeded in ridding their private Parnassus of every strain of dirt and untidiness. Here, even the drifting leaves look as if they have too much freedom. Thirteen children once lived in these houses, but it is hard to visualize them at play.

For once, unhappily, the pale green slopes of Parnassus are marked with a darker dye. The police camera turns to examine the Garfield family's Mercedes in the driveway of no. 3. Roger Garfield, a merchant banker in his mid-fifties, sits in the rear seat, head leaning against the off-side stereo speaker as if to catch some fleeting grace-note. He is a large-chested man with a well-lunched midriff and strong legs that have spent agonizing hours on an exercise cycle. He has been shot twice through the chest with a small-calibre handgun. Almost as surprising, he is wearing no trousers, and bloodstained footprints emerging from the house indicate that he was shot while dressing after his morning shower. He somehow managed to walk downstairs and took refuge in his car. Perhaps his clouding mind still assumed that he would be driven to his office in the City of London.

But the Mercedes was going nowhere. Garfield's chauffeur had been shot dead a few moments after his employer. A white-haired man in a black uniform, Mr Poole lies face down in the bed of orange-tipped cannas beside the front door, cap still held in his right hand.

The camera pauses over him and then enters the house, following the bloody footprints through the open door. Garfield and his wife had made numerous trips to Hong Kong, and the rooms are filled with pieces of chinoiserie – large porcelain vases stand on the blackwood furniture, and there are pairs of Ming horses and jade figurines. Surprisingly, none have been disturbed, suggesting that the murderers had approached their victims without surprise. The housekeeper, Mrs West, lies shot below the marble mantelpiece in the drawing-room, interrupted while doing her dusting. In an upstairs bathroom the camera finds Mrs Garfield, a handsome woman in her late forties, slumped against the glass door of the shower stall, her yellow toothbrush still in her hand.

All trace of the Garfields' 16-year-old son, Alexander, had vanished. His bedroom, study and bathroom were undisturbed. Only in his mother's blood flowing across the bathroom tiles could be seen the smeared prints of Alexander's rubber-cleated shoes, left behind as he was seized and swept away by his abductors.

The police video continues on its grim and matter-of-fact way. The camera leaves Garfield seated in his Mercedes and gazes across the tranquil lawns at the next macabre tableau. As the two constables outside the

Reade house (no. 1, The Avenue), step back from the colonnaded porch the camera reveals the lavish interior of the property tycoon's home, so filled with French furniture and objets d'art that it resembles one of the larger rooms at the Wallace Collection. Yet not a glass cabinet has been rifled, not a Sèvres plate shattered, not an ormolu clock toppled from its pedestal.

Indeed, Mr and Mrs Reade sit at their breakfast table in the dining-room, lying back in their chairs at opposite ends of the lacquered oblong as if momentarily overwhelmed by the calm and richness of the life they have arranged for themselves. Both have been efficiently shot by assailants who have crept so close to them that the cutlery beside their napkins is undisturbed. Only the place settings of the Reades' daughters, Annabel and Gail, have been scattered to the floor as these orphaned children made a desperate attempt to resist their kidnappers.

The camera resumes its melancholy tour. By the time it reaches the third house, the Gropius-inspired home of a distinguished concert pianist, the sequence of entrances, deaths and exits begins to resemble a nightmare exhibition that will never end. House by house, the assassins had moved swiftly through the estate on that quiet June morning, killing the owners, their chauffeurs and servants, before abducting the 13 children. Husbands and wives were shot down across their still-warm beds, stabbed in their shower stalls, electrocuted in their baths or crushed against their garage doors by their own cars. In a period generally agreed to be no more than 20 minutes some 32 people were savagely but efficiently done to death.

However, as the film ended, with a visit to the

perimeter guard post where the second security officer had been killed by a single bolt from a crossbow, I was struck by the way in which Pangbourne Village remained aloof from this day of death. The owners of these elegant houses had been dispatched with the least damage to the fabric of their homes, as if the facades of professional and upper-middle-class life were their most solid and lasting substance.

Indifferent to the lives, and deaths, negotiated within its walls, Pangbourne Village would endure. Once the mystery of this mass-murder and kidnapping had been solved, a seemingly impossible task with which I had now been charged, a new cast of tenants would soon be recruited to fill these calm drawing-rooms. For some reason, as I left the viewing theatre and stepped into the traffic-filled clamour of a Whitehall evening, I gave a small shudder for those new arrivals.

Pangbourne Village
Having exhausted my central nervous system with the police video, I returned to my office at the Institute of Psychiatry and tried to calm myself by looking at the origins and creation of Pangbourne Village.

The small Berkshire town of Pangbourne lies five miles to the north-west of Reading and approximately 30 miles to the west of London. Despite its title, the Pangbourne Village estate was not built near the site of any former or existing village. Like the numerous executive housing estates built in the 1980s in areas of deregulated farmland between Reading and the River Thames, Pangbourne Village has no connections, social, historical or civic, with Pangbourne itself.

The chief attraction for Camelot Holdings Ltd, the architects and property developers, was the proximity of the M4 motorway, and the ready access it offers to Heathrow Airport and central London, an ease of access that might well have benefited the assassins and kidnappers. All the residents of Pangbourne Village worked either in central London or in the silicon valley of high-technology computer firms along the M4 corridor. Pangbourne Village is only the newest (completed 1985) and most expensive (the ten houses, all with swimming pools, projection theatres and optional stables, each sold for approx. £590,000) of a number of similar estates in Berkshire which house thousands of senior professionals – lawyers, stockbrokers, bankers and their families.

Secure behind their high walls and surveillance cameras, these estates in effect constitute a chain of closed communities whose lifelines run directly along the M4 to the offices and consulting rooms, restaurants and private clinics of central London. They remain completely apart from their local communities, except for a small and carefully selected under-class of chauffeurs, housekeepers and gardeners who maintain the estates in their pristine condition. Their children mix only with each other at exclusive fee-paying schools or in the lavishly-equipped sports clubs sited on the estates.

Pangbourne Village is remarkable only for having advanced these general trends towards almost total self-sufficiency. The entire estate, covering some 32 acres, is ringed by a steel-mesh fence fitted with electrical alarms, and until the tragic murders was regularly patrolled by guard-dogs and radio-equipped handlers. Entry to the estate was by appointment only, and the avenues and

13

drives were swept by remote-controlled TV cameras. All police officers concerned in the investigation agree that the penetration of these defences by a large group of assassins was a remarkable and, as yet, inexplicable event.

The Residents
I turned to the list of victims, going through the detailed dossiers which the Special Branch had compiled, in the hope that the identities of the murdered residents might suggest some elusive clue. The sets of photographs, entries from *Who's Who*, the photostats of birth and marriage certificates, share portfolios and bank statements, academic qualifications and honorary degrees passed between my hands, the records of gifted lives so brutally ended.

1 The Avenue. *Julian Reade*, 43, chairman, Reade Investments. *Dr Miriam Reade*, 41, ear, nose and throat specialist, Wimpole Street. *Shot*.
   2 daughters: Annabel, 16, and Gail, 15.
2 The Avenue. *Charles Ogilvy*, 47, Lloyds underwriter; hon. secretary, Pangbourne Polo Club. *Margaret Ogilvy*, 42. *Shot*.
   1 son: Jasper, 17.
3 The Avenue. *Roger Garfield*, 52, merchant banker. *Helen Garfield*, 47, proprietor, Pedigree Kennels, Windsor. *Shot*.
   1 son: Alexander, 16.
4 The Avenue. *David Miller*, 49, stockbroker. *Elizabeth Miller*, 46. *Electrocuted*.
   1 son: Robin, 13. 1 daughter: Marion, 8.

5   The Avenue. *Dr Harold Maxted*, 54, psychiatrist,
    Harley Street. *Dr Edwina Maxted*, 48, psychiatrist,
    High Street, Kensington. *Crushed by car.*
    1 son: Jeremy, 17.
6   The Avenue. *Margot Winterton*, 48, concert pianist.
    Richard Winterton, 57, director, Winterton
    Arrangements Ltd. *Shot.*
    No children.

1   The Hill. *Richard Sterling*, 49, chief executive,
    EduCable, Oxford-area TV franchise. *Carole Sterling*,
    42, former ITN newsreader. *Suffocated.*
    1 son: Roger, 15.
2   The Hill. *Andrew Lymington*, 38, chairman, Leisure
    Marine Ltd. Ex-racing driver, 1982 Western Australia
    powerboat champion. *Sheila Lymington*, 37, former
    professional ice-dance skater. *Shot.*
    1 son: Graham, 15. 1 daughter: Amanda, 14.
3   The Hill. *Ernest Sanger*, 57, chairman, Sanger
    Finance. Proprietor, Windsor World Theme Park,
    Slough. *Deidre Sanger*, 54, managing director, She-
    She Fashions, Brent Cross. *Shot.*
    1 son: Mark, 16.
4   The Hill. *Graham Zest*, 46, chairman, Zest Health
    Foods. *Beverly Zest*, 42, company secretary, Zest
    Health Foods. *Shot with crossbow.*
    1 son: Andrew, 16. 1 daughter: Emma, 15.

The most careful research into the backgrounds of
these murdered men and women has failed to reveal any
common factor that might prompt a wholesale attack.
The responsible character of the parents and the
generous quality of family life have been reconstructed

from the abundant testimony of those domestic servants who fortunately were absent on 25 June (a Saturday, and their day off for most of the staff). All testify that the murder victims were enlightened and loving parents, who shared liberal and humane values which they displayed almost to a fault. The children attended exclusive private day-schools near Reading, and their successful academic records reveal a complete absence of stress in their home lives. The parents (all of whom, untypically for their professional class, seem to have objected to boarding schools) devoted long hours to their offspring, even to the extent of sacrificing their own social lives. They joined the children in various activities at the recreation club, organized discotheques and bridge contests in which they took full part, and in the best sense were guiding their sons and daughters towards fulfilled and happy lives when they themselves were cut down so tragically.

The Murdered Staff
In addition to the residents of the ten houses, the following members of staff were also killed.

Mrs Margaret West, Mrs Jane Mercier, Miss Iris Neame, housekeepers. *John Collis, David Taylor, James Poole*, chauffeurs. *Krystal Werther, Olga Norden*, au pairs. *Arnold Wentworth, David Lodge*, tutors. *George Burnett, David Turner*, security guards.

All investigation into the Pangbourne Massacre confirms that not a single adult present in the estate on the morning of 25 June survived the murderous half-hour which began at approximately 8.23 a.m.

The Missing Children

I looked at the photographs of the 13 children, a group of thoughtful and pleasant adolescents smiling out of their school speech-day portraits and holiday snapshots. All attempts to trace their whereabouts have failed, despite computerized searches of their dental records, blood groups and medical histories. Four of the 13 were on courses of prescribed drugs (for hay-fever, asthma and tinnitus), five were receiving orthodontic treatment, and one was under nominal psychiatric care (Jeremy Maxted, 17, for bedwetting). Despite what was clearly over-zealous prescription by their physicians, the latter willingly confirmed that the 13 children were well-nourished and enjoyed robust good health.

Extensive scuff-marks, bloody handprints and shoe impressions that match the children's known shoe sizes indicate that almost all the children were present at the scenes of their parents' murders. However, no traces of their own blood were found, and the children do not seem to have been harmed.

I closed the files, trying to believe that the children were still alive. Given the task faced by the assassins, and the often complex and ingenious ways in which they had murdered their victims, the fact that they had apparently inflicted no harm on a large group of probably hysterical children suggested that hopes for them, however desperate, might well be justified.

The Massacre: Various Theories

After this melancholy parade of murder and kidnap victims, I turned to the various theories suggested by the senior Home Office committee charged with the investigation of the killings.

(1) *The Lone Assassin*

Michael Ryan and the Hungerford tragedy come immediately to mind, like the many similar multiple murders in Japan, the United States and elsewhere. These motiveless killings, in which solitary psychopaths run amok, shooting at unknown passers-by, offer an explanation for the Pangbourne Massacre. It seems remotely conceivable that a solitary assassin, perhaps with specialist SAS training in murder by strangulation, trip-wire and crossbow, might have entered the estate, killed the security guards and then moved through the ten houses, restraining the children before killing the adult occupants. He may then have returned to collect the children, perhaps driving them away to some secret destination where they remain at his mercy to this day.

Comment: all the evidence collected, from a shattered video in the Lymingtons' house recording an early morning film transmission, to the clock in the Maxteds' Porsche which stopped when the car was driven into the garage door, indicates that the murders were carried out almost simultaneously, within a period of time lasting as little as ten minutes. Several of the victims were killed by gunshots fired in the open air, and it is inconceivable that the intended victims did not flee the estate at the first sign of danger.

(2) *Thrill Killers*

An extension of theory (1), which answers some of the objections to the single-killer hypothesis. Is it possible that a group of Michael Ryans, perhaps five or six deranged members of a local rifle club, strayed into the Pangbourne estate, perhaps after an all-night drug-taking orgy? Challenged by the guards, they were then provoked into a chain-reaction of violence and murder.

Comment: all the investigating teams (CID, Special Branch, Army Intelligence and secret services) agree that the murders were carried out by a band of assassins numbering at least half a dozen and more probably ten to 12, working skilfully together to a tightly planned schedule. It is unlikely that a group of psychopaths could have collaborated to this degree, given their customary impulsive behaviour and taste for random brutality. Although several of the victims were killed in ingenious ways, none was subjected to gratuitous cruelty. Indeed, the deaths have the clear hallmark of deliberate and careful executions.

(3) *A Misdirected Military Exercise*

The suggestion has been made in the tabloid press and by backbench Members of Parliament that the Pangbourne Massacre was the tragic outcome of an unofficial military exercise, in which a group of inexperienced SAS trainees were directed to the wrong target. They may have believed that they had been parachuted into a Warsaw Pact country, lost their heads and then murdered the adult residents of the estate before taking pity on the children.

Comment: enquiries at the highest level within the War Office and the secret services fail to substantiate this theory. A large area surrounding Pangbourne Village was minutely searched, but there is no trace of military vehicles, tyre-tracks or helicopter exhaust on grass or foliage. None of the residents of the nearby estates reports any sightings of military units. The lawns and soft ground within the estate show no footmarks of athletic men or any signs of their equipment.

(4) *The Political Dimension: Foreign Powers*

The scale of the Pangbourne Massacre, the number of victims and the daunting task of controlling a large group of children together suggest the deployment of resources that only a foreign power could muster. Many of the murdered parents held senior positions in professions that brought them into frequent contact with foreign governments. The possibility exists of an elaborate act of revenge for unpaid debts or 'consultancy fees'.

Comment: exhaustive enquiries confirm that none of the victims was politically involved in any way. Their only contacts were with US and EEC governments, and the latter's willing collaboration in the police investigation rules out this possibility.

(5) *International Terrorism*

Ballistics analysis of the spent bullets and the curious collection of weapons used point to the possible involvement of an international terrorist group, perhaps the IRA or a disaffected assassination squad of Libyan professionals. But the absence of any trace left by such a group, as well as the abduction of the children, rules out this option. However, the example of Patty Hearst suggests that one of the older children may have been brainwashed by a maverick group, perhaps a successor to the Baader-Meinhof gang, the French Action Directe, or the Italian Red Brigades. This remains an outside but remote possibility.

(6) *Organized Crime*

At least two criminal gangs in the East End of London and one in Glasgow are capable of mounting the large-scale operation involved in the Pangbourne Massacre. The abduction of the children may be part of a mass kidnapping attempt that misfired. Alternatively, the massacre may have been a revenge killing by an international drug syndicate. But there is no suggestion that even one of the parents was involved in drug dealing, in the laundering of syndicate revenues through the London money markets, or in any other activities connected with organized crime.

(7) *The Parents as Killers*

Could one or more parents have killed the others, and then committed suicide? Possible motives include sexual jealousy, professional rivalry, or individual psychopathy. Could the appalled children, in a state of shock that has still not lifted, have then fled the estate, taking refuge in a remote property owned by one of the families? Curiously, for all their participation in group activities at the recreation club, the parents themselves did not mix socially, never invited each other into their homes, and seem to have known one another only as casual acquaintances. All the domestic staff agree that in the three years of the estate's existence there was not a single example of marital infidelity between fellow-residents, a remarkable tribute to the concepts of social engineering built into the estate's design.

(8) *The Domestic Staff*
Could disaffected members of the domestic staff – the chauffeurs, housekeepers, cooks and tutors – have turned against their employers? All the servants on leave (one, an elderly gardener, died of a heart attack on hearing of the massacre) were repeatedly interrogated, and far from showing resentment they all seem to have sincerely admired their employers, and were clearly happy to work for them.

(9) *Bizarre Theories*
There remain a few outlandish possibilities.

(a) A unit of Soviet Spetnaz commandos, targetted on the residential quarters of the NATO headquarters staff at Northwood, received an incorrect war alert order and were parachuted by error into the Pangbourne estate during the night of 24 June. They slaughtered the adult residents, assuming they were senior military personnel, then realized their error and abducted the children.

(b) An experimental nerve-gas projectile fell from an RAF or USAF military aircraft into the Pangbourne area and deranged a group of nearby residents who committed the murders. They then destroyed all traces of the children before suffering retroactive amnesia that erased any memory of the crime. Unaware of the murders they carried out, they have now returned to ordinary domestic life.

(c) The murdered residents and their children were, unknown to themselves, deep-cover agents of a foreign power. Their mission accomplished, the parents were 'instructed' to murder each other, and the children disappeared into the cellars of the foreign embassy before being spirited abroad.

(d) The parents were murdered by visitors from outer space seeking young human specimens.

(e) The parents were murdered by their own children.

Looking through this list, it struck me that all were as fanciful as each other. Some uniquely strange event had taken place at Pangbourne Village, and to find its source I needed to visit the estate myself.

A Visit to Pangbourne: 29 August

Needless to say, the visit proved more difficult to accomplish than I imagined. Two months may have elapsed since the murders, but popular interest in the tragedy seems even higher now than it was in the days immediately after 25 June, fanned by the popular press and by a series of sensational TV documentaries. Last night the BBC's Panorama programme even speculated that a group of long-term unemployed from the north of England had come down to the leafy Thames Valley in search of jobs, and had been provoked by the ostentatious display of privilege and prosperity into a spasm of murderous rage.

Far-fetched, perhaps, but seeing the large crowd around the entrance to Pangbourne Village I felt that the theory was almost plausible. The murders have attracted an army of sightseers, most content merely to gaze at the houses from the surrounding lanes or any convenient high ground. Scores of people, many equipped with binoculars and cine-cameras, are trudging across the front lawns of the estates, much to the annoyance of the residents. I even saw one man, with a tripod and telescopic lens, clambering onto a garage roof and being pelted with gravel by the outraged chatelaine, a ferocious blonde in her dressing-gown.

The police try to disperse the public – all this must be a field day for burglars out on reconnaissance – but most of their manpower is needed to protect Pangbourne Village. A crowd of some 200 sightseers was packed into the tree-lined avenue leading to the estate, and there were people actually perched among the branches of the poplars, some with canvas awnings around them, while others shouted abuse at the police below.

As I edged my car through this mêlée an over-excited young constable pounded on the roof and almost broke the windscreen with his fist. Despite my written authorization from the Chief Superintendent at Reading he was extremely reluctant to let me through.

I was rescued by a Sergeant Payne of Reading CID, a polite but rather taciturn character who is stationed permanently at the estate, and I suspect is working off some minor penance. He is well-informed about the case, in an off-hand and sardonic way, but most of his energies are devoted to controlling the spectators. When I parked my car by the gatehouse I noticed that the police were making full use of the closed-circuit TV system, whose severed cables they had replaced. A shirt-sleeved officer scanned the monitors, sitting at the chair where his predecessor, the murdered security guard David Turner, was strangled in a strange cat's cradle of wire and bamboo (a device used by the Viet Cong to trap and kill American soldiers, so Sergeant Payne informed me).

Seeing the lawns, drives and front porches on the screens, I queasily remembered the police video I had watched in the Home Office theatre. As I stepped out along the well-bred gravel of The Avenue into the silent estate, surrounded by the impassive mansions, I half-expected to come across the Mercedes with a trouserless Roger Garfield in its back seat. Fortunately, the forensic teams have long since removed all evidence, and virtually erased every grim trace of the murders. The broken window-panes have been replaced, bloodstains chemically lifted, bullet-holes plugged and replastered. Even the lawns have been cut, on the instructions of the firms of solicitors representing the next of kin.

Walking around the estate, a bored Sergeant Payne 20 paces behind me, I found it easy to imagine that I was one of the prospective buyers visiting Pangbourne Village soon after its completion. The noise of the distant crowd was lost behind the high screens of rhododendrons, and the fine houses gave off the unmistakable scent of over-sleek contentment that comes from the combination of money and taste.

Selecting it at random, I walked up the drive to the Millers' house, no. 4, The Avenue. David Miller, a stockbroker, had been killed in his bath, his wife Elizabeth electrocuted on her booby-trapped exercise cycle. Their daughter, Marion, aged 8, and their son, Robin, aged 13, were the youngest of the Pangbourne children. While Sergeant Payne searched through his keys, I noticed the remote-control camera mounted on an art nouveau lamp standard in the centre of The Avenue. It turned towards us, the officer in the gatehouse keeping an eye on our comings and goings, and then swung away to scan the silent pathways between the houses.

I pointed to the camera. 'I must get one of those for my cottage at Pagham. They're useful things to have around.'

'Not useful enough.' Payne pushed the door open for me, unimpressed by the cameras. 'As it happens . . .'

'Of course, Sergeant. I only meant that they help to keep out intruders. Though constantly living under those lenses must have been a little unnerving. The security is cleverly done, but the estate does seem designed like a fortress.'

'Or a prison . . .' Payne lit a cigarette and deliberately exhaled a coarse blue smoke at the white-on-white interior of the Millers' home. Its deep-pile white carpets, chromium and leather furniture seemed to aggravate him in some way. 'The dogs and cameras keep people out, but they also keep them in, doctor.'

'A pretty comfortable prison, all the same,' I rejoined. His tone irritated me, like the ash he scattered on the carpet. 'Who on earth would want to escape? There's space for the imagination to breathe here, Sergeant. Young imaginations – I'm thinking of those children.'

And trying not to think of the Millers' two children, I began a brief tour of the house. As I gazed at the pleasantly furnished bedrooms, the boy's with his bathroom and personal computer room en suite, I visualized the civilized and contented lives that the stockbroker and his family had led. There was nothing museum-like about this home – the skirting boards in the boy's bedroom were scored by the heel-marks of a healthy teenager. Sections of the striped wallpaper were pockmarked with old sticky tape from which a gallery of posters had hung. A wide range of interests was on display – there were a chessboard, shelves of intelligent paperbacks, the computer room and its video library of classic films like *Citizen Kane* and *Battleship Potemkin*.

'A bright lad,' I commented as we looked back from

the doorway. 'This was a happy child.'

'Happy? It was practically compulsory.' Payne smiled through a set of tobacco-stained teeth. 'With all this gear, anything else would have been a crime.'

'Perhaps, but it's not that lavish, Sergeant. It's just that there are no rubbishy toys here. Tennis racquets, skis, home computer projects – it's all very sensible.'

'Oh, it's sensible.' Payne steered me down the corridor to the parents' bedroom. 'That's one thing you can say about Pangbourne Village. It's all very sensible . . . and very, very civilized.'

At the time I thought this an odd choice of words, with the peculiar emphasis that Payne gave to them. We were staring at the Millers' bathtub, where a man had been put to death before his own children, first stunned by the hairdrier thrown into the water and then stabbed with a kitchen knife. I tried not to visualize the seething explosion of bloody water. This civilized mansion was a modern House of Atreus. I remembered the photograph of the Millers in the dossier, which showed a thoughtful, friendly man and his cheerful, good-looking wife. In the downstairs gymnasium where she died on the booby-trapped exercycle there had been a wall diary marking out the various activities shared with the children – the school reading assignments to be talked over, the hour set aside after dinner to discuss television programmes of mutual interest, the social events at the sports club in which the parents were taking part, the next round of the Pangbourne Village fathers-and-daughters, mothers-and-sons junior bridge tournament. Scarcely a minute of the children's lives had not been intelligently planned.

Without thinking, I reached out and held the electric

plug of a hairdrier that hung beside the wash-stand (its double, the actual murder weapon, had been removed). The floor-to-ceiling mirrors that lined the walls multiplied the images of myself and Sergeant Payne. He watched me in his broody way, like a teacher patiently waiting for a dull pupil to catch up with him.

I realized that he wanted me to imitate the assassin's actions. Refusing to let him outstare me, I pressed the plug into the child-proof socket. The spring-loaded pins required a double flick of the wrist, forcing me to lean across the wash-stand. I switched on the hairdrier, feeling the rush of warm air across my face and forehead, ruffling my hair. I listened to its whir, and watched the smoke from Payne's cigarette swirl and dance around us, as the water vapour must have swirled and danced on a June morning two months earlier. The mirrors had been spattered with blood, and whoever had put Miller out of his misery had seen endless reflections of himself receding to infinity down aisles speckled with red confetti, a true blood wedding.

'Satisfied, Sergeant?' Annoyed with myself, I switched off the drier and led the way from the house.

The Psychiatrists' Home

We crossed the silent avenue, watched by the monitor camera mounted on its ornate stand, and continued on our inspection. Sergeant Payne rattled his keys, like the gaoler of a luxury prison for the miscreant super-rich. I felt that he disapproved of the people who had once lived in these houses, resenting them not merely for their wealth but for the humane way they displayed it.

All the same, I was glad of the company of this bored

policeman puffing on his sour cigarettes, nodding at my comments without listening. Already I knew that he would not confide in me directly, and I needed to find some way of provoking him.

Fortunately, the Maxteds' house provided the opportunity.

By chance, the Maxteds were the two murder victims whom I had actually met, at a Stockholm conference in 1986. I remembered an elegant and professional couple, almost too self-controlled with their silk suits and hand-tooled personal pagers. Their smooth, downplayed Gestalt and Human Potential jargon reminded me uncannily of the Scientologists, with the same reassuring patter concealing a hardnosed, evangelical sell.

But their home seemed pleasant enough, furnished in the comfortably oak-panelled way still favoured by the more controversial psychiatrists. Avoiding the garage, where the Maxteds had been crushed to death under the wheels of their own Porsche, Payne and I set off on a tour of the ground-floor rooms, through the well-equipped gymnasium to the indoor swimming pool beside the tennis court. The bulletin boards displayed the same obvious pride in their son's academic and sporting achievements that the Millers' had shown, the same friendly homework reminders, the same recommended TV programmes and suggestions for further reading.

I noticed in the Maxteds' study that none of my own books had a place on the shelves, an A–Z of once-modish names from Althusser and Barthes to Husserl and Perls. Whether to soften, or emphasize, this rigorously fash-ionable image, there was a small television set on the desk beside the ink-stand, placed there like the ultimate adult toy.

'And this is the son's room?' I asked as we entered the bedroom of the 17-year-old Jeremy. 'You know, Sergeant, other people's homes always seem a bit strange, but these are rather odd houses.'

'No more than some I've seen.' Payne ignored my obvious ploy, well aware that I wanted to get him rolling, but he glanced at me with mild curiosity. 'In what way, doctor?'

'I mean that they're so very alike. Not the furniture and fittings, though even they aren't that dissimilar. It's the atmosphere, the sense of very ordered lives being lived here . . . almost too ordered.'

I strolled around Jeremy's bedroom, noting the desk-top computer, the surf board and swimming trophies, a line of cups that packed the mantelpiece.

'He must have swum miles in that pool downstairs. Jeremy was the bedwetter, if I remember – perhaps the parents didn't appreciate all the effort?'

'Oh, they appreciated it . . . never stopped, in fact.' Payne pressed the computer keyboard, tapping out a simple code. The screen lit up with a message dated 17 May 1988.

'47 lengths today!'

There was a pause, and then:

'Well done, Jeremy!'

I stared at this message from the parents as it glimmered on the screen, a brief show of electronic affection, all that remained of parents and child in this deserted house.

'My God . . . you mean the parents were wired up to

the children's bedrooms? There's something unnerving about that, Sergeant.'

'Isn't there, doctor? You're sitting here after finishing your homework, and suddenly the computer blips "Well done, Jeremy!" '

'Talk about surveillance of the heart. It's not just those cameras out there. Still, he must have been happy.'

A pair of water-skis protruded from a cupboard. I drew back the door and glanced through the drawers, which were filled with music cassettes, paperbacks and sportswear.

Then, under a pile of diving caps in the bottom drawer, I found a stack of glossy magazines, well-thumbed copies of *Playboy* and *Penthouse*. I showed the top copy to Payne.

'*Playboy*, Sergeant – the first crack in the facade?'

Payne barely glanced at the magazine. 'I wouldn't say so, sir.'

'Of course not. What could be more normal for a 17-year-old still prone to bedwetting? The Maxteds were enlightened people.'

Payne nodded sagely. 'I'm sure Jeremy knew that too, doctor. The copies of *Playboy* made good camouflage. If you want to find the real porn have a look underneath.'

I pushed back the diving caps and lifted out the top three magazines. Below them were a dozen copies of various gun and rifle publications, *Guns and Ammo*, *Commando Small Arms*, *The Rifleman*, and *Combat Weapons of the Waffen SS*. I flipped through them, noticing that the pages were carefully marked, appreciative comments written in the margins. Mail-order coupons were missing from many of the pages.

'The real porn? I agree.' I pushed the magazines back
into the drawer, covering them with the diving caps as if
to preserve Jeremy Maxted's secret. 'He probably be-
longed to a local rifle club. But I don't suppose his parents
would have approved.'

'You can bet your pension they wouldn't.' Sergeant
Payne was smirking to himself. 'Handling a firearm? To
the people in Pangbourne Village that would be worse
than molesting a child.'

'A bit extreme, Sergeant. In a way they could be right.
Hold on a second . . .'

I switched on the cupboard light. Around the skirting
board and the interior panels of the door were a series of
curious notches, apparently left by a gnawing mammal
with powerful incisors.

'Have you seen these marks, Sergeant? It looks as if a
small creature was trying to get out. Did the Maxteds
keep some kind of exotic pet?'

'Only in a manner of speaking.' Payne ambled to the
door and held it open for me as we left the son's room.
'Those marks are quite common on the estate.'

'What are they caused by? The forensic people must
have some idea.'

'Well . . . they haven't been able to agree.' We had
entered Dr Edwina's bedroom. Payne pointed to the
wooden frame of the headboard, where I saw a similar
pattern of fretwork. 'You'll find them all over the place, a
kind of dry . . . rot.'

He emphasized the words with cryptic pleasure, then
sat on the bare mattress and switched on the bedside TV
set.

I said, sharply: 'Sergeant, I must be getting on – you'll
have to miss the local race meeting.'

'This is their own private programme, doctor. There's no gambling on the Pangbourne channel.' Payne pointed to the screen, which revealed the road outside the window. The camera tracked to and fro, as if searching for a fallen leaf, tirelessly hunting a panorama as silent as a stage set.

I shrugged at the screen. 'Security was important here, they were obviously obsessed by it. So the house has an input from the monitors at the gate?'

'Every house in Pangbourne Village.' Payne spoke in a droll but meaningful way. 'Upstairs and downstairs. At least we know why there were no infidelities here. But think of the children, doctor – they were being watched every hour of the day and night. This was a warm, friendly, junior Alcatraz. Swimming at eight, breakfast eight-thirty, archery classes, origami, do this, do that, watch the *Horizon* repeat on the video together, well done, Jeremy . . .' Payne blew his coarse cigarette smoke at Dr Edwina's dressing-table mirror. 'The only surprise about these people is that they found time to get themselves murdered!'

'Well, they were murdered. Let's not forget that.' I let Payne's outburst subside. He was still holding something back, and I waited to draw him out. 'But they certainly led very busy and well-organized lives. In fact, it's remarkable that the killers found them all in.'

'Perhaps they made an appointment.'

'By staging some pretext? It's hard to visualize what, exactly. Remember, this was a Saturday morning in June. It's quite a coincidence that no-one was on holiday. Between them these people owned about 15 properties, in the South of France . . .'

'. . . Cortina, Corsica and Tuscany.'

'All those places you hate, Sergeant. Yet everyone was here, every adult and every child. One of the children – Roger Sterling, the 15-year-old – was due to have his wisdom teeth out and was brought home for the weekend from the London Clinic.'

'Brought home?' Payne beckoned me into the ground-floor study as we spoke, still leading me on in all senses. 'Or did he volunteer, doctor?'

'Volunteer? Maybe. But for what? The diaries and appointment books show nothing – there were the usual Saturday activities – gymnasium work, the next round in the bridge contest, swimming . . .'

'. . . 47 lengths today! Well done, Jeremy!'

Ignoring Payne, I pressed on, reciting from memory. 'There was a visit by a TV producer planning a film about Pangbourne Village, a repeat of the *Panorama* programme on the Eritrean famine which a lot of the parents were watching with their children, and the disco in the evening. Nothing out of the ordinary . . .'

'But the boy, Roger Sterling made a real effort to be here. The London Clinic wasn't keen to let him go.'

'Right – he made up some story about a visiting friend from Canada who didn't exist. But why? Could the children have been planning a surprise?'

I was standing with my back to Payne, glancing at the books on the Maxteds' shelves, and waited for the Sergeant to reply. When I turned, a volume of Piaget in my hand, he was smiling primly, like a prudish man forced to enjoy the point of a vulgar joke.

'Yes, there's no doubt in my mind, doctor. The children were planning a surprise.'

'It's possible . . . and whatever their motive, the killers got wind of this. Correct?'

'I would say so.'

'Which suggests that they could plan the murders down to the last detail, confident where everyone would be. One thing is plain to me, Sergeant. The killers knew their way around.'

'Oh, intimately.' Payne sat back expansively in Dr Maxted's leather armchair, as if resting after work well done. 'The killers knew everything about the place, every staircase and jacuzzi and diving-board, every alarm switch and electric socket. But then they'd been here for years.'

'Years? But who, Sergeant? The servants?'

'No, not the servants.'

'Then who else? You sound as if you know.'

I gestured with the book in my hand, and it fell open awkwardly to reveal a broken spine. I stared down at the pages, many of which had been stabbed with the same dowelling tool that had damaged the skirting board in Jeremy Maxted's bedroom. Someone had gone through the book systematically mutilating its pages. Suddenly I guessed whose fingerprints would be found on the bruised end-boards.

'Sergeant, are you saying . . . ?'

'What do you think, doctor?'

'I've no ideas – but you obviously have.'

'One or two. I can tell you, they aren't popular.'

'Let's have them. I can cope with unpopularity.'

Payne stood up, composing his reply to me, but then strode to the window. A speeding police car swerved across the road and pulled up at the bottom of the drive, scattering the gravel. A uniformed inspector hurried across the grass. He pushed through the door, a look of triumph on his face.

'Sergeant, get back to Reading – you won't find anything here.' He turned to me. 'Doctor Greville, we have the Miller girl! The first of the children has escaped!'

Marion Miller, the First 'Hostage'
During the next week I remained at my consulting rooms at the Institute of Psychiatry. I saw those patients whom I had briefly neglected, and tried to keep my head down as an immense barrage of publicity greeted the discovery of Marion Miller. This tragically orphaned eight-year-old had been found in the early hours of 29 August, hiding in a skip loaded with overnight mail on Platform 7 of Waterloo Railway Station. A ticket inspector coming on duty (Frank Evans, 18 years' service with British Rail, already a national hero), had heard what seemed to be a cat hissing among the mail-bags in the skip. Trying to rescue the stray, he found the shivering and grimy form of a barely conscious child with matted blonde hair, wearing a bedraggled cotton frock and a single shoe.

The British Rail police were called, but the child, who was seven or eight years old and well-nourished, was unable to give her name. Exhausted by her ordeal, she was sunk in a state of speechless immobility, now and then emitting a strange hissing noise, as if she were imitating a pet cat. She was then handed over to officers of the local Metropolitan Police. They assumed that she was either a runaway or had been abandoned by her parents. A close inspection of the girl's clothing revealed a Harrods label in her cotton dress and the monogram of an exclusive Beauchamp Place outfitters in her single brogue.

A more significant finding was the series of stains of

organic origin, in the approximate pattern of the girl's left and right hands, on the waist of the dress. An attempt had been made to wash the stains from the fabric, but analysis soon showed them to be blood. The girl herself bore no injuries, and by eight o'clock that morning speedy identification revealed the blood to be that of David Miller, one of the victims of the Pangbourne Village Massacre. Shortly afterwards, dental and photographic evidence, and the visual confirmation of both grandmothers, established that the girl was Marion Miller, one of the 13 abducted children.

During the next few days the discovery of this orphaned child swept all other news from the media, which became a vast pressure cooker of speculation fuelled by the uncertainty over the circumstances of the girl's release. Had she escaped, or was she the first of the children to be set free by the kidnappers? All the 1980s love of 'hostages' soon transformed the 12 remaining children into pawns in a sinister game played with their lives and hearts by the unknown kidnappers. Several national newspapers established ransom funds, which received millions in public donations.

The child herself was unable to help, lying in her closely guarded ward at the Great Ormond Street Children's Hospital, and in an irreversible state of catatonic seizure. She was sedated and fed by tube, but on meeting her grandmothers during her brief conscious moments she could merely hiss and make a strange movement of the left hand, as if unlocking a door, while touching her forehead with her right hand, presumably to ward off a blow.

This seemed to confirm that the child had escaped. The

skip in which she had been found contained mail-bags from the Canterbury area – had a fanatical religious order seized the children, perhaps a group of deranged high churchmen opposed to the liberal archiepiscopal establishment? Marion's dress had been washed with a popular brand of detergent retailed for a soft-water area in Wales – Welsh nationalists came under immediate suspicion, and holiday cottages in the principality were sold off by the score. Meanwhile her single brogue contained soil traces from Kensington Gardens, which were ruthlessly scoured as if Peter Pan, now grown into an Ian Brady-like psychopath, had returned from never-never land and beguiled the children into his evil dream.

However, all these speculations soon faded into the air. There was no word from the kidnappers, and Marion Miller remained locked in her deep withdrawal. I requested permission to see the child, and attached a brief report of my visit to Pangbourne, in which I described certain curious features, such as the mutilated copy of Piaget's classic text on the rearing of children. The Home Office turned me down, asking me to discontinue my investigation and hold myself indefinitely in reserve.

Left alone, I was able to think again about my visit to Pangbourne Village and my talk with the cryptic Sergeant Payne, who had now been redeployed to one of the task forces roaming the country. He had seemed to point to the complicity, deliberate or otherwise, of Jeremy Maxted in the abduction of the children and even, perhaps, in the murders themselves. Had Jeremy's secret passion for military weapons led him to purchase a rifle or handgun, which had then provoked the kidnappers into killing the parents?

Meanwhile, the eight-year-old Marion Miller remained the only key to the tragedy, but she showed no signs of recovery. My own interest waned, and I returned to my work with my patients.

Then, wholly by chance, in one of the TV documentaries that I liked to despise, I saw a brief film of the child. This rekindled all my interest in the case and settled in my mind, for once and for all, the mystery of who had killed the 32 victims of the Pangbourne Massacre.

The Television Film

The TV film, yet another *Newsnight* recapitulation of the tragedy, introduced a short sequence recorded at the Great Ormond Street Children's Hospital. The police had allowed the cameras into the ward for the first time, as part of their now desperate appeal for witnesses of the child's escape.

Marion lay in her bed, her clenched fists pulling the sheet to her pursed lips. Her head rested to one side, torpid eyes apparently staring at the vase of irises on the nearby table. An elderly woman, the maternal grandmother, dressed in a Persian lamb coat and carrying a patent leather handbag, was guided to the bed by a nursing sister. She smiled hesitantly at her granddaughter, as the sister moved the flowers on which the child had fixed her gaze and urged her to turn her head.

My hall telephone rang while I was watching this affecting scene on the television screen. I paused at the door of the living-room, as Marion Miller stared at the imposing figure of her grandmother. In a now famous gesture, endlessly repeated on TV and even mimicked by alternative comedians, the child raised her left hand from the safety of the sheet. She seemed to press a key into a lock and then turn it with a difficult double motion of her small hand – exactly the sequence of wrist movements, according to the experts, that would release a spring-loaded mortice lock. At the same time her right hand rose to her forehead, as if warding off the blow of one of the kidnappers, probably on the other side of the door and between whose legs she had made her brave and miraculous escape.

Confirming this theory, the child's mouth was set in a frightening rictus. She exposed her clenched teeth, parting her lips in an ugly grimace as her incisors gleamed against the camera lights. Although there was no sound-track, every one of the millions of viewers must have heard the hiss.

While the telephone continued its weary ringing, I walked to my TV set and turned down the reporter's commentary. I stared at the orphaned child's wounded and desperate eyes, and at her pinched little face under the lovingly brushed blonde hair, knowing that I had identified at least one of the Pangbourne murderers.

Return to Pangbourne Village: 17 October 1988
Sergeant Payne was waiting for me at the gatehouse, when I arrived at eleven o'clock the next morning. He gave a patient salute, but showed no emotion on seeing me. Even on the telephone he had been noncommittal, as if unsurprised by my urgent call. The keys to the Millers' house in his hand, he steered me through the onlookers who still gathered at the gate.

Together we strode through the silent estate, past the

handsome mansions which I already saw in a very different light. The familiar interior of the Millers' house greeted us, yet every perspective had subtly changed. Payne stood aside, waiting to see which way I would turn.

'The parents' bathroom,' I told him. 'That's all we need to see.'

'Very good, doctor . . .' Payne spoke encouragingly, an instructor guiding a promising recruit through an obstacle course. But when we reached the bathroom I was at last able to surprise him.

'Let me set the stage, Sergeant.' I pulled open the shower curtain and turned on the bath-taps. 'We need one or two props . . .'

Payne stepped back, trying to avoid his multiplying images in the mirror walls. 'If you're thinking of taking a bath, doctor, the heating's been turned off.'

'Don't worry, I won't embarrass you.' When there were two inches of cold water in the tub I turned off the taps, then took Mrs Miller's hair dryer from its stand above her wash-basin. Holding it in my hands, I turned to Payne.

'Now, Sergeant, you saw the television film of Marion Miller, apparently unlocking a door as she made her escape. She was certainly escaping, but not by turning a key . . .'

For the first time I was ahead of Payne. He watched me cautiously, an unlit cigarette between his lips, as I transferred the hair dryer to my right hand and held the plug in my left.

'So, let's assume that Miller was taking a bath that Saturday morning. At about 8.15 Marion and her brother come into the bathroom. Perhaps they ask a special favour, the answer to which they already know, a last chance for their father to save his life.'

'Doctor . . .' Payne was shaking his head, clearly disappointed in me. 'That's pure speculation.'

'All right, I'm guessing there. But of this bit I'm sure.' I placed the hair dryer on its stand above Miller's wash-basin. 'Marion picks up the hair dryer and plugs it into the socket. To do this she has to step around the edge of the basin and reach forward with her left hand. Sadly for the father, these child-proof sockets aren't quite child-proof enough . . .'

I pushed the plug into the socket, then made the familiar turn, press, turn again motion which the stricken child in the TV film had made so memorable. The hair dryer whirred into life, blowing hot air across my face.

'She's now holding the dryer in her left hand by the pistol grip – it's difficult to hold the thing any other way – and there's a rush of air that blows her fringe into her eyes. She pushes it away with her right hand . . .' I made the second gesture that we had seen in the film, smoothing down the few hairs that danced across my forehead.

Then I stepped back and tossed the hairdrier into the bath. There was a violent hiss, and a muffled flash that jolted the sides of the bath, lighting up the mirrors around us. Scalded water spat across Payne and myself, spraying fine drops across the ceiling.

Its fuse blown, the hair dryer lay inertly below the seething water. I switched it off at the socket and disconnected the plug. Payne was drying his jacket with one of Mrs Miller's face-towels.

'You heard the hiss, Sergeant – something that poor child will never forget. In fact, it's probably the last thing she remembers.'

'I won't forget it either, doctor.' Payne gingerly lifted the hair dryer by its cord from the bath. 'To be honest, I hadn't worked out the plug business, but I knew she wasn't opening a lock.'

'Of course not. Why should that have traumatized her? Only an overwhelming crisis would have buried itself so deep in her mind, something that involved matters of life and death, or beyond life and death.'

'Like deciding to kill her father?'

'Exactly – though I don't think she did kill him, and she may well know it. She stunned him with the hair dryer, and her brother then killed him with the kitchen knife.'

Payne leaned over the bath-taps and released the water from the tub. 'So you think they planned it? The brother and sister together?'

'Yes, they planned it, just as all the murders at Pangbourne Village were planned. You know that, Sergeant. In fact, you've known it ever since my first visit here.'

'That leads to another question, doctor. *The* question – who actually carried out the Pangbourne Massacre?'

'The children, without any doubt. It sounds so outlandish, I'm not even sure if I believe it myself. There's no proof and we may not find any. All the same, I'm certain that the Pangbourne parents, one by one, were killed by their own children.'

We stood in the dripping bathroom, surrounded by the endless images of ourselves, listening as the last trickle of water ran away through the house.

Uneasy with his own reflection, Payne said: 'I agree, doctor, but it's hardest to prove right here, in this bathroom. An 8-year-old girl and her 13-year-old brother? You'll have a merry time making that one stick.'

'Perhaps, but I'm sure that Robin and Marion Miller are the key to everything. Remember, they were the youngest of the 13 children, and they had a particular problem that none of the others faced. Their father was a huge man, well over six feet tall, a former amateur boxer. The boy would never have been able to stab him fatally.'

'And if he'd only wounded Miller he'd have been able to warn the other parents?'

'Very likely – the parents were intelligent enough to realize that something serious was amiss, and rapidly draw the right conclusions.'

'Like lock the nearest doors, don't switch on that appliance, decide *not* to walk in front of the car when the teenage son is staring at you in a funny way over the steering wheel. The whole operation could have unravelled . . .'

'Within minutes. So young Robin and Marion Miller faced a double challenge. They had to move quickly, and they had to kill their parents themselves.'

'But why, doctor?' Payne had managed to relight his wet cigarette, and sucked hungrily at the smoke. 'One of the older boys, the Ogilvy lad or the psychiatrists' son, could have done it for them.'

'That would have destroyed the whole moral basis of the exercise. The children were making a last stand against their parents. The Pangbourne Massacre was a desperate rebellion, from the children's viewpoint, an act of mass tyrannicide. Each one had to take responsibility for the death of his own parents, whatever the cost.'

'They certainly put a lot of ingenuity into it – all these electrical booby-traps, these strange nooses and harnesses. At first that pointed to a really sick professional killer.'

'I thought so too, Sergeant – but the ingenuity here was born out of necessity. The younger children had never seen a firearm, let alone handled one. The murders had to be carried out in a very short period, perhaps no more than ten minutes, to keep up the psychological momentum. They had to be fast, and they had to be efficient.'

'It's no good a 13-year-old boy walking up to his mother in the kitchen and trying to stab her.' Payne shook his head, pondering upon this grim spectacle. 'Just think of all that jogging. Those Pangbourne mothers were a collection of fit women, they'd spent a lifetime fighting off young men. Even a fatal stab wound might give them a chance to raise the alarm – especially those alarms that ring inside the head.'

'The loudest kind. Imagine trying to kill someone who loves and cares for you, Sergeant. The murder act has to take place so quickly that you haven't time to think.'

'First time and dead on time. That meant planning, doctor. It's hard to believe the children could have brought it off themselves.'

'I know. All the same, Sergeant, I'm certain that they acted alone. I think they murdered their own parents at about eight o'clock that Saturday morning, without the help of anyone else. They probably left Pangbourne Village within a few minutes of the murders, perhaps in a rented bus parked around the corner.'

'And now?'

'Who knows? I dare say they're sitting it out in some quiet country farmhouse in a remote corner of Wales or Scotland.'

'They'll be mothering a goat, planting carrots, and lying awake all night as they wait for the dawn chorus. And we'll never hear from them again.'

'Oh, we'll hear from them again, Sergeant. One act of tyrannicide leads to another, especially with this emotional charge behind it. The Pangbourne children are a Baader–Meinhof gang for the day after tomorrow. That's why we've got to make our case against them as strong as we can before we go to the Deputy Commissioner.'

'I won't comment on that, doctor.' Payne drew the shower curtain, as if concealing a still-visible corpse. 'But one last question. I agree the children killed their parents, and that they carefully planned it together. But why? There was no evidence of sexual abuse, no corporal punishment getting out of control. The parents never raised a hand against the children. If there was some kind of tyranny here it must have been one of real hate and cruelty. We haven't found anything remotely like that.'

'And we never will. The Pangbourne children weren't rebelling against hate and cruelty. The absolute opposite, Sergeant. What they were rebelling against was a despotism of kindness. They killed to free themselves from a tyranny of love and care.'

The Pangbourne Massacre: the Evidence
The next three days I spent almost entirely in Sergeant Payne's company, assembling our detailed case against

the Pangbourne children, a case that challenged every-thing held most dear by conventional good sense, but which needed to carry total conviction if it was to overcome the reflex objections of the Yard and the Home Office.

Each morning I drove from London to the Reading police headquarters, and Payne would take me down to the archivist's office in the basement where the classified evidence was stored. Although I was certain of our case, once away from Pangbourne Village I found it difficult to accept the strange logic at work – that the more the children were loved and cherished, the more they were driven into a desperate search for escape.

'Take Marion Miller,' I pointed out, playing devil's advocate against myself. 'I'm convinced that she drop-ped the live hair dryer into her father's bath. All the same, the inference that she set out to kill him deliberately is so bizarre that one has to look at the possibility of other bizarre theories.'

'Such as, sir?' Payne waited patiently by the projector screen with the collection of slides and videos he had assembled.

'Well, perhaps she wanted to dry his hair for him, and dropped the hair dryer into the water by accident. She panicked, and the brother tried to make it look like a suicide attempt. Perhaps it *was* a suicide attempt which the children blundered into . . .'

'So Miller first electrocuted himself, to shut out the pain, and then stabbed his own chest?'

'Or perhaps the mother stabbed him, and then in remorse killed herself – ?' I gave up. 'It's implausible, but our theory is even more unbelievable.'

'At least it explains the other murders. Let me show you this tape, doctor.' Payne switched on the projector. 'This comes from the TV monitor in the gatehouse. It contains the final sequences before the system was sabotaged at 8.23 a.m. – the main cable and all the telephone lines were severed with a set of cutters stolen two weeks earlier from a British Telecom van in Reading.'

The video revealed a general view of The Avenue on the fateful morning, the lawns and pathways deserted, the residents in bed, at breakfast, or taking their fateful baths. 'It's now about 8.22, according to the time coding on the tape. David Turner, the security guard in the gatehouse, was probably strangled within 30 seconds of the tape ending. The audio-cassette in his breast-pocket radio records the unanswered query of Burnett, the other guard on duty, who was calling from the perimeter security post about the camera failure. Something like 30 seconds later *he* was killed by a crossbow bolt.'

'And these two deaths started off the whole Pangbourne Massacre?'

'That's what everyone upstairs assumes, all the senior CID people and the Yard. According to them, this was the signal to the other members of the gang waiting to attack.'

'It seems likely – someone had to fire the starting pistol.'

'Sure. But let's run the tape back a little, doctor . . .'

The pictures moved in reverse, showing the familiar perspectives of the estate, except for a solitary pigeon that flew tail-first down The Avenue, as if withdrawing tactfully from the tragic scene. At Pangbourne Village, I reflected, time could run backwards or forwards. The residents had eliminated both past and future, and for all their activity they existed in a civilized and eventless world. In a sense, the children had re-wound the clocks of real life.

'This is the Miller house.' Payne pointed to the graceful modern facade. 'It's now about 8.19, and the Millers are ready for another rich and successful day to wrap itself around them.'

I ignored this and watched the screen. The surveillance camera, as if bored with nothing to do, began to scan the house in close-up. The superb lenses, representing the most advanced optical technology, showed every detail with unnerving clarity. The camera panned along the plate-glass windows of the lounge and dining-room. The undisturbed furniture could be clearly seen, even a clock registering 8.20 on a mantelpiece.

'Nothing untoward there,' I commented. 'No assassins waiting for a signal . . .'

'Hold on, doctor – you'll see the assassins in a moment.'

The camera passed the study windows. The darker background of bookshelves concealed the interior, but somewhere in the confused play of light and shadow I saw the image of a child.

'Wait, Sergeant! Hold it there.'

'You saw it, doctor? Good . . .' Payne froze the frame and enlarged the image. Marion Miller was standing on a chair by the window, her knees against the sill. Her untidy blonde fringe partly covered her eyes, but on her lips was a small tight smile, unmistakable in its fierce knowingness. Her gaze was fixed on one of the houses across The Avenue.

Behind the girl was her brother Robin, his face dappled

by the reflected foliage. His eyes also watched the house opposite. Between the two children was the desk-top screen of the security monitor.

'It's the same picture that you and I are watching,' I pointed out to Payne. 'Perhaps they've seen something, Sergeant, and they're trying to warn everyone . . .?'

'No, they're just waiting for the screen to go blank. It's this little pair who fire your starting pistol.' Payne ran the film in slow motion. Marion's brother had come to the window beside her. Boy and girl clasped hands and raised them over their heads in a gesture reminiscent of a black power salute.

'Look closely at this, doctor . . .' As the smiling girl lifted her arm she pressed against the window, and her dress flared across the glass. Imprinted on the waist were two floral patterns like stylized tulips.

'Handprints, doctor. They were still there when she was found at Waterloo Station, in the same blood group as her father's.'

I stared at the five-fingered patterns. 'Fair enough, Sergeant. So at this point Miller and his wife were already dead. Robin and Marion were first off the mark, and then came downstairs to signal to the others. Everything depended on whether these two were up to it.'

'It's easy to follow their line of sight. They were looking across The Avenue at the upstairs window of Annabel Reade's bedroom. She must have passed on the message to whoever cut the TV and telephone cables.'

'Then all the screens went blank, and the killing machine rolled into action.' I walked over to the projector, fascinated by the flower-shaped prints of the child's hands. 'So that's where she wiped her fingers – I can see her doing it as her brother finishes off the father in the bath. But what about the people at the Yard? How do they explain this?'

'They don't try. They say the boy and girl had been locked into the study and were signalling for help.'

'For heaven's sake, she was smiling – an icy smile, I admit, but a smile.'

'Enough to freeze the lips off the Mona Lisa,' Payne commented. 'A tough little lady. If she was strong enough to start everything off, why did she want to escape?'

'Because she was so young. Everyone else had reached puberty, they were choking on the non-stop diet of love and understanding being forced down their throats at Pangbourne Village. This was an idea of childhood invented by adults. The children were desperate for the roughage of real emotions, for parents who now and then disapproved of them, became annoyed and impatient, or even failed to understand them. They needed parents who weren't interested in everything they did, who weren't afraid to be irritated or bored by them, and didn't try to rule every minute of their lives with the wisdom of Solomon.'

'And Marion Miller?'

'She was only eight – at that age you enjoy being cocooned in total affection, with someone telling you what to do every moment of the day.' I tapped the softly glowing image of the smiling girl. 'She fired the starting pistol, but she wasn't the ringleader, and perhaps she began to remember the happy paradise she had left behind at Pangbourne. Let's go through the other material, Sergeant – older and far more dangerous heads planned the Pangbourne Massacre.'

The Pangbourne Children

During the next hours Sergeant Payne, using film, slides and videos, took me through the evidence assembled by the police investigation into the characters and history of the Pangbourne children. Together it formed the portrait of a group of likeable and talented youngsters, successful at school and with a wide range of outdoor interests that included swimming and hang-gliding, scuba-diving and parachute-jumping. As I looked at the photographs of these fresh-faced teenagers, snapped by their friends as they posed in their flying overalls and wet-suits, I could not help thinking that all these activities involved the element of escape, as if the children were unconsciously equipping themselves with the means to break free from their lives.

Surprisingly, however, their interest in these outdoor sports had begun to lapse during the previous year, as the children moved the focus of their activities to their own homes. This was clear from their diaries and videos, and from the private newspaper, oddly named *The Pangbourne Pang* (circulation, 13 copies) published from his desk-top printer by the 15-year-old Roger Sterling. A darker and more closed world soon emerged.

By the winter of 1987 the children had abandoned their hang-gliding and scuba-diving, and were spending nearly all their time in their own rooms. So gradual was this process that it was scarcely noticed by the domestic staff, though in their testimony two of the maids commented on the increasing difficulty of cleaning the children's quarters.

Miss Rogers: He was building a strange kite, that completely filled his whole bedroom. Once I tried to pick it up and it just snapped shut around me. Mark had to cut me loose – he was very sorry, and Mr Sanger asked him very nicely to apologize.

Mrs Stacey: Graham was always playing with his computer, adding up all these numbers. Finally I had to ask Mrs Lymington to put my times on the bulletin board.

This loss of interest in outdoor activities inevitably led to the withering-away of their friendships with children from the nearby estates. Fewer school-friends visited them, and those who did commented on the clannish atmosphere.

William Knox, 14, school-friend of Roger Sterling: They were busy with their own thing. It used to be fun there, and then it wasn't fun any more.

Philip Bax, 15, son of a Reading doctor: It wasn't really spooky, but they seemed to have gone away. They used all these codes talking to each other.

This retreat within the perimeter of Pangbourne Village appears to have been unplanned, but the secret hobbies of the children might well have given the parents pause. The milder of these, like the rifle magazines concealed in Jeremy Maxted's cupboard, lay well within the bounds of ordinary adolescent behaviour. Almost all the children kept diaries, either written in longhand or typed into their word processors, and most were either shredded or erased in the days before the massacre.

However, two of the girls, Gail and Annabel Reade, kept elaborate secret journals which were discovered in the panels behind their dressing-table mirrors. These throw no direct light on the Pangbourne murders, but describe a richly imagined alternative to life in the estate that at the same time seems an implicit comment upon it.

The journals cover the lives of a number of genteel Victorian families living in Pangbourne in the late nineteenth century, a caring and affectionate upper-middle-class community described in a formal prose reminiscent of Jane Austen but with a startling frankness about their sexual activities. Together they convey the impression of *Pride and Prejudice* with its missing pornographic passages restored. Two of the charming and well-bred daughters establish themselves as prostitutes and serve the desires of the other members of their families of whatever sex and age. Yet it is clearly not the pornographic details that appeal most strongly to Gail and Annabel – these are sketched in perfunctorily – but rather the powerful emotions which their sexual passion elicits. What comes through most vividly is the sense that through these sexual activities the over-civilized inhabitants of Pangbourne can make their escape into a more brutal and more real world of the senses.

Many of the other hobbies of the Pangbourne children show the same obsession with the theme of escape. Andrew Zest, an enthusiastic radio ham, had rigged a powerful radio antenna on the roof of his house and was trying to communicate with intelligent life in a neighbouring galaxy. This complex array of wires was only discovered when it interfered with the estate's TV security system.

The same reductive strain was apparent in *The Pangbourne Pang*, desk-top printed by Roger Sterling and distributed between March and June 1988 to its 13 readers. In a lively tabloid visual style, it specialized only in boring news. 'Egg boils in three minutes' and

'Staircase leads to second floor' are two of its banner headlines.

Graham Lymington, meanwhile, programmed his computer to calculate pi to a million places, and papered the walls of his bedroom with the print-outs. Gently dissuaded from this by his parents, he then put out *Radio Free Pangbourne*, a cassette audio-programme, six issues of which were distributed to the other children in November and December 1987. This was a sequence of random sounds, mostly his own breathing, interspersed with long patches of silence.

The key to all these was the curious home video, filmed by Amanda Lymington and Jasper Ogilvy, which at first sight appeared to be a matter-of-fact documentary of daily life at Pangbourne Village. Some 17 minutes long, it was made with the happy cooperation of the parents, and adopts the style of a real estate developer's promotional video. With its glossy colour and tableau-like settings, it depicts the parents sitting in their drawing-rooms, having dinner, parking their cars. The commentary is warm and affectionate, and the film is a light-hearted parody, before the event, of the BBC-TV documentary which was to be made about Pangbourne Village in the late summer of 1988. There is a certain gentle leg-pulling at the parents' expense – the camera lingers on Mrs Sterling as she mistimes a swallow dive, and on Mr Garfield as he drops his cocktail shaker.

Extracts of the film were shown to the parents and often screened for the benefit of visitors. However, the final version that secretly circulated among the children was very different. This carried the identical jovial sound-track, but Jasper and Amanda had added some 25 seconds of footage, culled from TV news documentaries, of car crashes, electric chairs and concentration camp mass graves. Scattered at random among the scenes of their parents, this atrocity footage transformed the film into a work of eerie and threatening prophecy.

Almost all copies of the video tape were destroyed at some time before 25 June, but a single cassette was found in the Maxteds' bedroom safe. One wonders what these fashionable psychiatrists made of it. Seeing the film, I had the strong sense, not for the first time, of young minds willing themselves into madness as a way of finding freedom.

'It's a remarkable piece of work, Sergeant,' I said to Payne as the film ended. 'I can't help feeling that it links everything else together.'

'Could the Ogilvy boy have been the ringleader? He was the oldest of them.'

'Possibly – something acted as the trigger, and persuaded the children to plan the murders.'

'The film, doctor. It's practically a detailed blueprint for the killings – shootings, car crashes, electrocutions . . .' Payne grimaced, almost gagging on his own cigarette smoke. 'It's as if the film came first for them.'

'By the time they made this everything was turning into a film. The BBC producer was due to visit the estate on the afternoon of June 25. Perhaps the planned documentary was the last straw – the children knew they'd have to play their parts for the cameras, doing all the interviews, acting out their "happiness" under the eyes of their doting parents. The prospect of all that phoniness could have driven them over the edge . . .'

I walked to the projector screen, which showed the cryptic credits of the children's video, 'A Pangbourne Village Production', superimposed upon an idyllic view of the estate. I was thinking of Marion Miller – if I was right, her escape had been a desperate attempt to return to her childhood world.

'Tell me, Sergeant, could you get me an edited version of the video?'

'Without the car crashes and electric chairs? I can arrange one for you, doctor. Who do you want to show it to?'

'Marion Miller. It's just an idea. It might help to remind her of happier times.'

The Great Ormond Street Kidnapping

Needless to say, Marion Miller was never to see the film. During the next two weeks, as I waited for the Home Office to reply to my request, she continued to lie in her guarded room at the Children's Hospital in Great Ormond Street. She had made friends with her nurses, murmuring and lisping like the three-year-old version of herself to which she had reverted. I assumed that she had blotted out all memories of the days leading up to the Pangbourne Massacre and the murder of her parents.

Sensibly, I kept my suspicions to myself, and said nothing to the Home Office of my belief that the 13 children were not the assassins' victims but were themselves the killers. No trace of them had been found, despite a marathon of manhunts organized by the police and national newspapers. No ransom note or list of demands had been sent to the authorities, and the 12 missing children had effectively vanished into another continuum.

Two of them, however, were nearer to hand than anyone had imagined.

Early on the afternoon of 4 November I walked

through the lobby of the Children's Hospital with the video cassette in my briefcase. I had not been given permission to show the film to Marion, but while talking to an assistant commissioner at Scotland Yard I learned that the child was watching videos of children's programmes on the television set in her room.

When I arrived, I found that two uniformed police officers were guarding the private ward on the fourth floor. They examined the video without comment, and my Home Office pass saw me into the child's presence. A young nurse was sitting beside the bed, laying out a jigsaw on a metal tray.

Marion Miller watched me quietly with a thumb in her mouth. Blonde curls hid her small forehead, and her overlarge eyes made her resemble a dreamy infant scarcely off the breast. Could this vulnerable child have murdered her own father and set in train the Pangbourne Massacre? For a moment my faith in my own theory faltered.

'Look, Marion – doctor's brought a film for you.'

The nurse put aside the jigsaw, but Marion had already noticed me. As she turned her head a sharp blue eye surveyed me through the blonde fringe, and I could only too well imagine her father's disbelief as this demure parricide dropped the hair dryer into his bath.

Was she aware that I was avoiding her eyes? Busying myself with the television set, I engaged the nurse in small talk, letting her insert the cassette into the video player.

When I switched on there was a sudden clamour of noise from the corridor outside the ward. I assumed that the volume control of an extension speaker had been incorrectly set. Then there were the sounds of a violent scuffle, and the ringing clatter of an overturned trolley. The door into the ward burst open. One of the uniformed constables stepped backwards into the room, reaching for the revolver in the holster under his tunic.

Through the open door I could see the trolley lying on its side, enamel kidney basins scattered across the floor. A terrified orderly was on her knees against the wall. The second policeman tried to help the woman, disguising his right hand as he drew his revolver.

He was looking up at his assailants, two small figures in white gowns and face-masks, their T-shirts incongruously bearing a pop group's logo, whom I took to be a pair of undersized laboratory technicians. However, each held an automatic pistol. Like trained dancers they side-stepped past the debris on the floor. The policeman in the corridor began to raise his revolver, when there were two hard, rapid reports like fuses blowing.

Shot through the chest, the policeman lay at the intruders' feet as they stepped into the ward. Above the masks their eyes glanced at the television set, which was now showing the Pangbourne Village film. I heard the second constable shout a warning, and then a brief volley of shots jarred the windows. The constable stepped forward to the door, one hand raised like a blind man feeling his way, and collapsed onto his knees.

The next few seconds passed in a confusion of sudden violence. The intruders moved to Marion's bed, weapons raised as if about to kill the child. I stepped forward to protect her, but one of them bent down and lifted Marion from the bed, pressing her face against his shoulder. The other had removed her mask, revealing the white, stony face and aroused eyes of a teenage girl. She moved to the window, and glanced into the street. As she searched the passing traffic I saw a revolver in the right hand of the nurse – in fact, Special Branch officer Doreen Carter. There was a last exchange of gunfire that tore an oblong of jagged glass from the window. Wounded in both arms, officer Carter dropped her weapon to the floor and crouched against the bed.

As the kidnappers fled with the child, pausing at the door to fire a last shot at myself, I recognized them as Annabel Reade and Mark Sanger of Pangbourne Village.

It was some minutes later, when the ward filled with police, security staff and emergency medical teams, that I switched off the television set. The screen was wet with blood, and I realized that I had been shot in the left hand.

The Pangbourne Massacre: the Murderers Identified
During November, as I convalesced from the wounds to my wrist and palm, I had ample time to replay in my mind that terrifying scene at the Great Ormond Street Children's Hospital. Discussing the episode with a CID superintendent, we came to the conclusion that the entire assault had taken no more than 20 seconds, from the overturning of the trolley to the kidnappers' flight with Marion Miller. In this time one uniformed police-man had been killed, a second constable and the woman Special Branch officer seriously wounded. Detective Carter's intervention almost certainly saved my own life – it seems probable that the kidnappers intended to shoot both of us after disposing of the police guards.

Their ruthless efficiency confirmed that the kidnapping had been carefully planned. No trace has been found of the gang, and we can only guess whether Marion Miller is still alive. The suggestion that two of the Pangbourne children were responsible met with strong resistance, both at the Home Office and in the national press. Too much emotional capital had been invested in the notion of the 13 orphaned children.

However, Annabel Reade and Mark Sanger have been repeatedly identified, not only by officer Carter and myself, but by the nurses and doctors of the two wards to which these murderous adolescents had been admitted for observation. They had arrived three days before the kidnapping, apparently referred to Great Ormond Street by the casualty department of a north London hospital. This gave them ample time to survey the security and layout of the building, and the exact location of Marion Miller. As children they were never challenged, a problem which would have faced any adult kidnappers.

Interestingly, they left their fingerprints all over the furniture and utensils in their wards, and this suggests that they are fully prepared to admit their part in the kidnapping and, by implication, in the murder of their own parents. However, I would guess that the children are now far beyond the point where questions of guilt and responsibility have any meaning for them.

Is Marion Miller still alive? The assumption at the Home Office and Scotland Yard is that she will have been killed, before she could reveal the whereabouts of the gang, and that the kidnap was in fact a botched execution. Needless to say, I am confident that Marion is alive, and that the nightmare logic of the Pangbourne Massacre demands this. Just as the older children required Marion to play her part willingly in the murder of her parents, so they need her now to believe in the rightness of their cause. Fanaticism of that kind is rooted in total unity. Besides, the older children must realize that within a year or two at the most, when she ceases to be a young child, they will have won Marion forever.

A Tentative Explanation

A spate of fresh theories has been offered to account for the murders, many of them variants of earlier theories that the children are the agents of a foreign power or have been brainwashed by advanced hypnotic drugs. There is even the suggestion that the massacre was a misguided rehearsal of the murder of the Kremlin Politburo by their own grandchildren, which would be triggered in the event of a nuclear war.

The Home Office dismisses all these, and points instead to the Jonestown Massacre. It believes that the children came under the sway of one of the older adolescents, a Manson-type ringleader who exerted a messianic hold over the others, seducing them by the force of his warped personality. The murder of their parents was the initiation rite that led to membership of his deranged cult. The Home Office is confident that, sooner or later, the gang will break cover as they forcibly recruit new members, or as the leader's megalomania carries him over the brink into delusions of omnipotence.

I doubt this. There is no sign that any of the older children was a ringleader, or that any kind of coercion was ever employed. Despite the desk-top newspapers, cassettes and videos which they circulated, the Pangbourne children tended towards solitary pursuits. Thanks to the television cameras and their crowded recreation schedules, the children were virtually prisoners in their own homes.

My own view is that far from being an event of huge significance for the children, the murder of their parents was a matter of comparative unimportance. I believe that the actual murders were no more than a final postscript to a process of withdrawal from the external world that had begun many months beforehand, if not years. As with the Hungerford killer, Michael Ryan, or the numerous American examples of crazed gunmen opening fire on passers-by, the identity of the victims probably had no special significance for them. More than this, I would argue that for such killings to take place at all, the deaths of their victims *must* be without any meaning.

By a grim paradox, the instrument of the parents' deaths was the devoted and caring regime which they had instituted at Pangbourne Village. The children *had* been brainwashed, by the unlimited tolerance and understanding that had erased all freedom and all trace of emotion – for emotion was never needed at Pangbourne, by either parents or children.

Denied any self-expression, and with even the most wayward impulse defused by the parents' infinite patience, the children were trapped within an endless round of praiseworthy activities – for nowhere were praise and encouragement lavished more generously than at Pangbourne Village, whether earned or not. Altogether, the children existed in a state closely akin to sensory deprivation. Far from hating their parents when they killed them, the Pangbourne children probably saw them as nothing more than the last bars to be removed before they could reach out to the light.

I often think of Annabel Reade and Mark Sanger at the Great Ormond Street Hospital, and of their toneless faces as they turned their weapons on us. I remember the experiments in sensory deprivation that I attended at the School of Aviation Medicine at RAF Farnborough, and the great dangers to the laboratory staff presented by these deeply desensitized volunteers. The attempt to help them from their sound-proof immersion tanks could be fraught with risk. On numerous occasions the volunteers had injured themselves and even attempted to strangle the laboratory staff while under the impression that they were warding off stray equipment that had intruded into their zero world.

The same schizophrenic detachment from reality can be seen in the members of the Manson gang, in Mark Chapman and Lee Harvey Oswald, and in the guards at the Nazi death-camps. One has no sympathy for Manson and the others – an element of choice existed for them all – but the Pangbourne children had no such choice. Unable to express their own emotions or respond to those of the people around them, suffocated under a mantle of praise and encouragement, they were trapped forever within a perfect universe. In a totally sane society, madness is the only freedom.

The Trigger
In the cases of Michael Ryan, Mark Chapman and Oswald one can assume that the unconscious decision to commit their crimes had been taken many weeks before the actual event. What provided the trigger for the

Pangbourne children? This will not be known until the children are captured and interrogated, if ever. Nonetheless the planned arrival of the producer of the TV documentary on 25 June may have warned the children that time was running out. The programme researchers and the fashionable sociologist who would front the documentary had also agreed to visit the estate, and had already spoken to the older children.

The last issue of *The Pangbourne Pang* reveals that the provisional title of the documentary was 'The New Samoa', a reference to Margaret Mead's influential but partly discredited work in which she described the idyllic world of these unrepressed islanders, from whose lives all jealousy, repression and discord had been erased. The prospect that this glib sociologist would soon take up virtual residence at Pangbourne for the three months of the programme's filming may well have spurred the children into action.

Another factor may have been the reports, well-advertised in the architectural press, that the 'success' of Pangbourne Village had led to plans for the construction of similar estates nearby, and that within two or three years these would be amalgamated in a super-Pangbourne with its own schools, community clubs and resident youth counsellors, protected by even more elaborate security systems.

At all events, the children must have known that they had only a few days to act before they were enrolled into the documentary. Intensely proud of Pangbourne Village, the parents were all present on 25 June, presumably to meet the TV team. How the children planned the massacre is not yet known, but it is possible to reconstruct the last hours leading up to the murders, with the help of a few imaginary interpolations.

25 June 1988 – The Reconstruction
5.56 a.m. The first sighting of one of the children on the morning of the massacre. A surveillance camera picks up the night security officer Edwards as he walks down The Avenue, on his way to the gatehouse. He has made his final circuit of the estate. At 6.00 he and officer Baines will hand over to their two replacements on the day shift. As the camera follows Edwards it catches the 17-year-old Jasper Ogilvy watching through the transom window of his bathroom.

Jasper's slim, child-like face is composed, but he has a lot to do. At 6.00 Mark Sanger, who can see the gatehouse from the laundry-room window of the Sanger home, will signal that the guards' changeover has taken place. On Saturday morning the replacement shift is often late, and the men will then make tea together in the gatehouse, subtracting 15 minutes from the next two crowded hours. During this time Jasper must see that the three children on his roster (Marion and Robin Miller, and Annabel Reade) are awake and ready for action, then slip out and retrieve the shotgun he has buried behind the rose pergola. He must return to his bedroom with the weapon, before joining Mark Sanger in the task of cutting the telephone and TV cables.

6.02 a.m. Mark Sanger also has a full two hours. In addition to cutting the cables with Jasper, he has to supervise the three children on his alarm roster (Andrew and Emma Zest, and Roger Sterling). Most difficult of all, he must assemble the lethal bamboo man-trap, still masquerading as a box-kite, which hangs from the ceiling of his computer-room, and carry it across the open lawn under his parents' bedroom. Officer Turner is a stickler for security, and Mark knows that he will only gain access to the gatehouse by using a decoy. In this case the decoy *is* the murder weapon.

Leaning on the pile of linen sheets below the window, Mark impatiently watches the gatehouse. He knows that he is nowhere near so self-controlled as Jasper, or the slightly creepy Roger Sterling, but he is surprised by the sweat pouring from his arms onto the linen sheets (Exhibit 75). Where are the security men?

6.09 a.m. Annabel Reade listens to the alarm under her pillow. In the dim light of the bedroom she sees the paging signal blinking softly on the computer screen. Jasper is calling her, tapping out the opening lines of her favourite book, *Animal Farm*. She must remember to erase the signal before they leave. Switching off the alarm, she gets out of bed, unsteady but refreshed, and glad that Jasper insisted they all have a night's sleep. Through the wall she can hear that her sister Gail is awake. She types in the acknowledgement signal, 'Snowball', and goes into the bathoom, leaning with her palms (E 98) against the mirror as she is sick into the basin (E 99). There is no time even to wash or brush her teeth. After dressing in her blue tracksuit she begins to unscrew the aluminium baffle of the ventilator shaft above the computer. Already she can see the slide and barrel of the two Remington pistols which she and Gail will use to kill their parents.

6.15 a.m. By now all the children have risen, alerted by their own alarms and the paging signals on their computer screens. Graham Lymington has slept fully dressed, and is already waiting by his terminal as the awake signal appears on the screen. Next door, his 14-year-old sister Amanda has a shower, using her nightdress to block the drainage grille between her feet (E 63), so that her parents will not hear the pipes drumming.

Only Jeremy Maxted has been unable to sleep – he has spent the night in his bedroom armchair, watching an all-night TV channel with the sound turned down. He disturbs the bed, but its dry and uncreased sheets confirm that it has not been slept in.

Emma Zest has risen at 4.00 a.m., and spends the next two hours sitting in her brother's bedroom, watching him as he sleeps, his crossbow in her arms. One of its steel bolts slips below the cushion (E 29), but there are nine others, more than enough for both their parents and the perimeter security guard Burnett.

Marion Miller is also up and dressed before her brother, and sits on the edge of Robin's bath, eating a chocolate bar as he uncoils the electric cable which she has hidden inside her doll's house and which he will plug into the steel frame of their mother's exercycle.

Roger Sterling, Graham and Amanda Lymington are in visual contact with Jeremy Maxted across The Avenue, and duck to avoid the security camera on the weather vane as it pans across the houses. Roger is late – in his excitement the previous day he dropped his alarm clock, and he wakes at 6.05 to see the paging signal pulsing fiercely on his computer screen. He breaks a shoelace of his jogging shoes and stumbles noisily across the bedroom, but he knows his parents cannot hear him.

In their nearby bedroom they are in a deep, drugged sleep from which they will never wake.

6.21 a.m. The security day shift has arrived! Fortunately there is no time for tea. The wait has been exhausting for Mark Sanger – the sheets in the linen-room are sodden with his sweat – but the moment Baines and Edwards drive off, taking the two loathsome Dobermans with them, he feels an immense relief. He has always feared the dogs, which are only allowed onto the estate at night (all pets are discouraged at Pangbourne Village; they foul the lawns and are a distracting focus of affection). He watches Turner and Burnett settle into the gatehouse, and then signals to Jasper Ogilvy. The first of the parents will begin to rise between 7.00 and 7.15, and this gives the children barely 40 minutes to move around the estate.

6.23 a.m. Jasper leaves his bedroom, closing the door behind him. There is no sound from his father's bedroom, but he waits outside his mother's door, listening to her deep, uneven breathing, which occasionally breaks into a snore. She is often awake for a few hours in the middle of the night, but then sleeps deeply until well after dawn. Jasper walks across the landing and opens the cabinet of the burglar alarm system. He disconnects the electrical circuit that links the windows and doors together during the night. As he eases the toggle his sweaty hands leave ample fingerprints (E110) on the plastic handle.

Jasper is now free to leave the house. He enters the silent kitchen, unlocks the outer door and lets himself onto the patio behind the garages. Screened by the roof of the swimming pool from his parents' bedrooms, he sets off across the lawn. Behind the rose pergola he retrieves the buried shotgun, which he carries back to the house and hides among the golf clubs in his bedroom cupboard.

He then returns to the garden. Beyond the tennis courts, the rear gate opens onto the pathway inside the perimeter fence, which Burnett will patrol in 20 minutes. Jasper sets off along the path until he sees the gatehouse on its grassy knoll, separated from the houses by a screen of ornamental trees. Jasper parts the hanging curtain of a weeping willow. Squatting against the tree-trunk is Mark Sanger, the bamboo man-trap on the ground beside him.

6.35 a.m. Andrew Zest is moving through the trees at the bottom of The Avenue, near the pathway at the northern perimeter of the estate. This is the furthest point from the gatehouse, and the surveillance camera sweeps the lonely pathway for a full hundred yards on either side. Attached to the pylon is a telephone box and a miniaturized relay from the gatehouse of the camera picture.

Behind the pylon is a dense mass of rhododendrons, their dark leaves shutting out all signs of the houses. Graham crouches within the foliage and unpacks the crossbow from his canvas satchel. Using the spanner, he cranks back the powerful bow. His feet slip in the soft earth as he fits a steel bolt into the runnel. He carefully rearranges the foliage, satisfied that he is only six feet from the telephone box.

6.48 a.m. Mark and Jasper expose the telephone and TV cables. Over the past week they have excavated a rectangular pit in the damp soil, cut through the tar-paper housing and the yellow plastic tubing that contains the cables. Jasper lowers the steel cutters into the pit. Beside him Mark is setting the springs of the man-trap, bending the bamboo arms that will pinion officer Turner and allow him to strangle himself.

7.00 a.m. The children's preparations are now complete. Graham Lymington has taken the bolt-action target rifle from beneath the floorboards in his bedroom. In the grey light he cuts his right thumb on the loosened nails (E 42). He sits on the bed, cleaning the weapon for the last time, then feeds the soft-nosed cartridges into the magazine.

Annabel and Gail Reade have completed the last exchange of messages on their computer screens. Annabel has loaded her small Remington and left the pistol within reach in the drawer of the bedside table. Gail has placed her weapon between the legs of her teddy bear. Sitting on the beds in their separate bedrooms, the two girls can see Jeremy Maxted at his window across The Avenue, reading an American comic that he has smuggled into the estate.

Composed now, the children wait in their rooms, computer screens glowing and blank, ready for the action to come.

7.05 a.m. The first parents begin to wake. Mrs Sanger lies in bed for a few minutes, making notes for the day into the tape recorder of her bedside radio-clock. 'The TV people will be here at three. See the garage this morning about the spare car-key. Ask Miss Neame to prepare the lobster dressing. Cancel riding lesson, and check with Mark about his weekend programme . . .' (E 142).

7.12 a.m. Charles Ogilvy writes down a dream on the bedside telephone pad (E 159). He has dreamed of sailing down the Nile, a journey he and his wife made three years earlier, but in his dream the great temples and pyramids have been replaced by film sets . . .

7.29 a.m. Margot Winterton plays the radio in her bathroom and records an interesting film review on Radio 4's morning magazine programme.

7.45–8.00 a.m. All the parents are now up and awake, with the exception of the Sterlings, who are still drugged by the powerful sleeping draught which Roger managed to steal during his visit to the London Clinic. The living-in tutors, Mr Lodge and Mr Wentworth, and the two au pairs, Krystal and Olga, have also risen. Several of the parents exercise in their bedrooms before bathing, while others don tracksuits and jog around their swimming pools.

8.05 a.m. Mrs West, the first of the domestic staff to arrive, parks her small Honda in the rear drive of the Garfield house. Two more domestic staff appear, Miss Neame and Mrs Mercier, both intrigued by the expected visit of the TV unit, as their relatives testify. They busy themselves taking the mail and newspapers which they have collected from officer Turner at the gatehouse. They prepare breakfast and switch on the dishwashers.

8.10 a.m. The children wait. Weapons are loaded, and where necessary appliances have been booby-trapped, lethal electric cables plugged into their sockets. Hidden within the willow tree, Mark and Jasper kneel beside the exposed telephone and TV cables, cutters in hand. The children's attention is now on the Miller house.

8.15 a.m. At about this time Mrs Miller, relaxed after ten minutes of tai chi, mounts the exercycle in the family gymnasium. Overhead she can hear her husband running the water for his bath. Her children, as far as she knows, are still in bed, and she is tempted to prepare a little surprise for them. She settles herself on the well-sprung seat of the exercycle. Its powerful electric motor will rotate the pedals while rocking the seat and handle-bars, and she has to take care to stay on. She slips her feet into the pedal straps and sets her hands onto the metal grips with their leather cuffs. Cables run from the motor to the power socket on the wall. There are many electric cables in the gymnasium, to the scales, sunbed and rowing machine, and Mrs Miller fails to notice the extra cable that runs from the positive terminal of the motor and is clipped to the steel frame of the cycle between her legs.

She reaches down and switches on. Immediately a 32-amp charge surges through her body, galvanizing every muscle and almost throwing her from the machine, but she is held to the bucking seat by her ankle and wrist cuffs. Perhaps in the wall-length mirror she catches a last glimpse of Marion and Robin, watching quietly from the open door as her arms and legs, head and torso gyrate wildly on this last ride.

Three minutes later, the father lies in his bath, listening to the curious slapping sound from the gymnasium (his wife's right leg striking the floor). When his son and daughter enter the bathroom he asks them about the noise, but through the steam he sees his daughter plugging the hair dryer into its socket. She brushes her blonde fringe from her eyes and walks up to the bath, looking at him with a strangely fixed smile.

8.21 a.m. Annabel Reade sees Marion and her brother waving from the Millers' study. The signal moves swiftly to Mark and Jasper, waiting with their cutters beside the exposed TV and telephone cables. In their bedrooms, the children sit quietly, each with a telephone receiver to the ear. Some 90 seconds later the lines go dead.

8.23 a.m. Within the next seven minutes all the remaining adults in Pangbourne Village meet their deaths.

Puzzled by the blank monitor screens in the gatehouse, officer Turner goes out to inspect the camera mounted on the roof. Mark Sanger is waiting outside the door, with another of the box-kites he is always building, but Turner is too busy to speak to him and waves him into the office. When Turner re-enters the gatehouse Mark is standing by the lavatory door. Burnett is calling on his radio-pager, reporting that the perimeter camera seems to be dead. Turner sits at his desk and looks down at his monitors, vaguely aware that Mark has stepped behind him, still talking about his kite. The boy raises it into the air, demonstrating how he will fly it. There is a sound of string snapping, and suddenly Turner is gripped around the throat and chest by a powerful vice. He has a glimpse of bamboo-green arms, as if he has been seized by a giant praying mantis.

8.25 a.m. Dr Harold and Dr Edwina Maxted are walking to their car, which is parked in the rear drive behind the garage. They have a busy day ahead of them. Dr Edwina has a hair appointment in Reading, and Dr Harold must collect the Super-8 camera with which he will record his conversation with the TV producer. They are pleased that Jeremy has reversed the black Porsche out of the garage for them before returning to his breakfast. Its engine ticks softly in the crisp morning air.

Dr Edwina notices that her son has left a magazine on the gravel by the garage doors. To her surprise it is a lurid American horror comic. She points it out to her husband, and Dr Harold stands beside her, nodding thoughtfully as she lifts it in her well-manicured fingers. Neither sees their son sitting up in the driving seat of the Porsche, and they barely hear its engine as it leaps across the gravel towards them.

8.26 a.m. Officer Burnett strides along the perimeter path towards the emergency telephone. The pivot of the pylon camera has jammed, and he has called Turner on his radio-pager without success. Burnett reaches the telephone beside the rhododendrons. The miniature screen is blank, and all the electrical systems have broken down. He opens the cabinet and is taking out the receiver when the first of the crossbow bolts strikes him in the back.

Julian and Miriam Reade are having breakfast under their Louis XV chandelier. Their daughters, Gail and Annabel, enter the dining-room. They are wearing their tracksuits and smile in a conspiratorial way, hands held behind them as if bringing a surprise present for their parents. Annabel stands behind her mother, Gail behind her father, asking them to close their eyes. Sitting there, they are shot in quick succession through the backs of their heads.

8.27 a.m. Roger Garfield, the merchant banker, is dressing in his bedroom. He listens to his wife talking in the bathroom, when his son Alexander opens the bedroom door. In his right hand is a small calibre automatic pistol. Alexander raises the weapon, as if showing his father something he has found, and then shoots him through the chest. Mr Garfield sits down on the bed, barely able to breathe, and presses his hand against the blood leaking through his white linen shirt. He tries to speak to his wife, who is backing through the bathroom door. Her son's second shot misses her, but she falls across the bidet and he shoots her twice in the head as she lies half-stunned against the glass door of the shower stall.

Ignoring his wife and son, Mr Garfield walks from the bedroom onto the landing, blood running down his trouserless legs. Alexander is a few steps behind him, but Mr Garfield is thinking only of the Mercedes parked outside the front door. There is just time for Poole to drive him to Reading Hospital. When he opens the door he speaks to the chauffeur, Mr Poole, who has heard the muffled sounds of the shots and has left his chamois leather and polish on the roof of the Mercedes. Before the chauffeur can go to the car-telephone Alexander follows his father into the open sunlight. The chauffeur steps into the flower-bed, but Alexander shoots him down among the flame-tipped cannas.

Still ignoring everything except the numbness in his chest, Mr Garfield climbs through the passenger door of the Mercedes and sits in his rear seat. A disc jockey is talking on the car radio, but the words mean nothing to Mr Garfield and the sound is soon drowned by the last of the shots which his son fires at him through the passenger window.

8.28 a.m. Mark Sanger has returned home from the gatehouse. The razor-sharp wires of the man-trap had cut his left hand as he dropped the spring-loaded frame over officer Turner, and he pauses by the bottom of the staircase to wrap the wound in his handkerchief. His mother comes out of the library, where she has been standing by the window with Mark's father, puzzled by the distant sounds of the Porsche colliding with the doors of the Maxteds' garage, and by what seem to be muffled gunshots around the estate. They have tried to call both the gatehouse and the Reading police, but the telephone line is dead. Concerned for her son, and surprised by his bloodstained tracksuit, Mrs Sanger fastens her dressing-gown and walks up to him, but he ignores her and runs up the stairs to his bedroom. She is half-way up the long flight when he re-appears by the balustrade with the pump-action shotgun he had hidden among his golf clubs.

8.29 a.m. Also puzzled by the muffled gunfire and the dead telephone lines, the Wintertons open their front door. Jeremy Maxted is standing by their Volvo estate wagon, and they assume he has come to clean the car, one of the voluntary good-neighbour tasks which the Pangbourne parents have persuaded their children to carry out. Reassured by Jeremy's quizzical but ready smile, Mrs Winterton goes to her kitchen to collect a bucket of water and a wash-leather. When she returns to the hall she finds her husband lying on the doormat. She can see that he is dead, but she kneels down to loosen his collar. It is only then that she notices Jeremy standing in his bloodstained sneakers in the doorway of the cloakroom.

8.30 a.m. By now all the remaining adults in Pangbourne Village are dead. Only Richard and Carole Sterling die in their own bed together, still deep in their drug-induced sleep and unaware that their son Roger is suffocating them with their pillows. The three housekeepers are shot down as they hurry to their cars. The last to die, the tutor Mr Wentworth, had taken refuge in the Lymingtons' library, and is shot dead by Amanda as he corrects her homework project.

Disappearance of the Children

Having murdered their parents and the other adults who stood in their way, the children vanished from the estate. They appear to have left within ten minutes of the last murder, and no clues have been found to their method of escape. Many of them were wearing tracksuits, and given the popularity of jogging in the Pangbourne area no-one would have been surprised by a party of jogging teenagers, while the drying blood would soon have resembled the mud-splashes of an arduous obstacle race.

Apart from the armed abduction of Marion Miller from the Great Ormond Street Hospital, there have been no sightings of the children. Bearing in mind the special nature of their crime, I assume that they will emerge again at some future date, probably in a spectacular attempt to assassinate a leading public figure. I have been unsuccessful in convincing the authorities of my fears. The inquest into the parents' death returned an open verdict, and to this day the Home Office believes that the children were abducted by their parents' murderers.

Postscript, 8 December 1993

Five years have passed since the Pangbourne Massacre, and the first news has been heard of the 13 children. During this time there has been no trace of the group, and Scotland Yard assumes that they are either dead or in the custody of a foreign power. The kidnapping of Marion Miller from Great Ormond Street is seen as part of this conspiracy, and it is assumed that the young murderers were either drugged or acting under duress.

Sergeant Payne and I are the only ones to remain sceptical. Payne has continued to send me whatever pieces of information come his way, but the special investigation unit of Reading CID has long since been disbanded.

However, he telephoned today to tell me that in the early hours of this morning an assassination attempt was carried out against a former British prime minister. All details of the affair have been hushed up, but it seems that an armoured truck was driven at speed through the gates of the house. The explosion that followed, on an exclusive estate in Dulwich, south-east London, has been attributed to a leak in a nearby gas main. The former prime minister was unharmed, and was photographed handing out cups of tea to the police and firemen. As before, she continues to enjoy respect, if not affection, as a leader now sometimes known as 'the Mother of her Nation', or 'Mother England'.

These titles, recently coined by a sycophantic newspaper editor nostalgic for the halcyon days of the 1980s, must have been a red rag to the Pangbourne children. The oldest of them is 22, and most of the others have left their adolescence behind. Even Marion Miller is now 13, and it is interesting that one of the former prime minister's bodyguards reported that the assault seemed to be directed by a stern-faced teenager with blonde hair which she brushed compulsively from her forehead. He speculated that these gestures might have been a set of coded signals.

Will the children strike again? I take it that all authority and parental figures are now their special target. So the regime of kindness and care which was launched with the best of intentions at Pangbourne Village, and which has prompted countless imitations in the exclusive estates of southern England, not to mention Western Europe and the United States, has given birth to its children of revenge, sending them out to challenge the world that loved them.